One Cool Friend

Story by Toni Buzzeo

Pictures by David Small

Dial Books for Young Readers an imprint of Penguin Group (USA) Inc.

For Ms. Joanne Stanbridge, one cool and unblinking friend,

whose love and laughter brought Magellan to his full glory —TB

To Edison —DS

DIAL BOOKS FOR YOUNG READERS
A division of Penguin Young Readers Group
Published by The Penguin Group
Penguin Group (USA) Inc., 375 Hudson Street, New York, NY 10014, U.S.A.
Penguin Group (Canada), 90 Eglinton Avenue East, Suite 700, Toronto, Ontario, Canada M4P 2Y3 (a division of Pearson Penguin Canada Inc.)
Penguin Books Ltd, 80 Strand, London WC2R 0RL, England
Penguin Ireland, 25 St. Stephen's Green, Dublin 2, Ireland (a division of Penguin Books Ltd)
Penguin Group (Australia), 250 Camberwell Road, Camberwell, Victoria 3124, Australia (a division of Pearson Australia Group Pty Ltd)
Penguin Books India Pvt Ltd, 11 Community Centre, Panchsheel Park, New Delhi - 110 017, India
Penguin Group (NZ), 67 Apollo Drive, Rosedale, Auckland 0632, New Zealand (a division of Pearson New Zealand Ltd)
Penguin Books (South Africa) (Pty) Ltd, 24 Sturdee Avenue, Rosebank, Johannesburg 2196, South Africa
Penguin Books Ltd, Registered Offices: 80 Strand, London WC2R 0RL, England

Designed by Lily Malcom
Text set in Stone Informal
Manufactured in China on acid-free paper
10 9 8 7 6 5 4 3 2 1

Library of Congress Cataloging-in-Publication Data

Buzzeo, Toni.
    One cool friend / by Toni Buzzeo ; pictures by David Small.
        p. cm.
    Summary: Elliot, a very proper young man, feels a kinship with the penguins at the
aquarium and wants to take one home with him.
    ISBN 978-0-8037-3413-5 (hardcover)
[1. Penguins—Fiction. 2. Etiquette—Fiction. 3. Humorous stories.] I. Small, David, date, ill. II. Title.
    PZ7.B9832On 2012
    [E]—dc23
                    2011021637

The art was done with pen and ink, ink wash, watercolor, and colored pencil.

Elliot was a very proper young man.

So on Saturday morning when his father said,

"Family Fun Day at the aquarium. Shall we go?"

Elliot thought, Kids, masses of noisy kids. But he only said,

"Of course. Thank you for inviting me."

At the aquarium, Elliot's father settled on
a bench to read his *National Geographic*.

"Have some fun, Elliot," he said.

So Elliot did.

He skipped the mobs of kids at the Giant Saltwater Tank,
Amazing Jellies Display, and Hands-on Tide Pool Exhibit.

HANDS-ON
Tide Pool

At the end of the hall, he discovered . . .

PENGUINS!

In their tidy black feather tuxedos with their proper posture, they reminded Elliot of himself.

Even Ferdinand Magellan
looked like his kind of guy.

Elliot emptied the school notices from his backpack, selected the smallest penguin,

and popped it inside.

In his room, Elliot dialed the air conditioner down to its coldest setting.

So Elliot dragged his old wading pool upstairs, then fed the garden hose through the kitchen window and turned on the faucet.

HMS. BEAGLE

"Forgive the inconvenience," he said as he passed his father's office.

Soon the air conditioner
had done its work.

Later, Elliot knocked on the door of his father's office.

"I have some research to do at the library about Magellan."

"When I was in third grade, I got Captain Cook," his father said.

"Where did you keep him?" Elliot asked.

But his father had already returned to charting the changing boundaries of the Great Barrier Reef.

Elliot and Magellan rode to the library.
When Elliot set him on the librarian's desk,
Magellan held completely still.
Ms. Stanbridge didn't blink an eye—even when
Magellan blinked his.

She helped them access www.PenguinsOnIce.com,
copy pages from *Antarctic Anecdotes*, and borrow
Best Behavior for Birds.

On the way home, Elliot stopped for eight bags of
ice and a snack. Luckily his father's twenty-dollar
bill was just enough to cover it.

Elliot read his library book aloud while Magellan cooled down. They shared a bag of Goldfish crackers, but Magellan was still hungry.

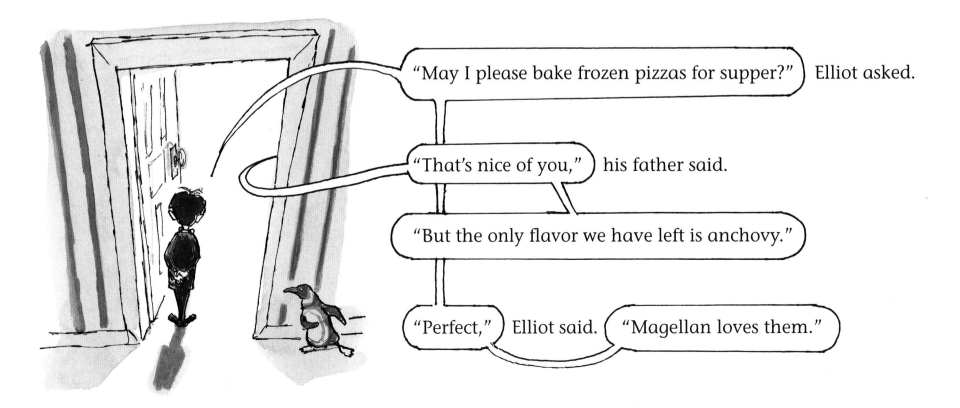

"May I please bake frozen pizzas for supper?" Elliot asked.

"That's nice of you," his father said.

"But the only flavor we have left is anchovy."

"Perfect," Elliot said. "Magellan loves them."

That evening, Elliot heard his father rummaging for ice cream.
Luckily, Magellan had politely moved the carton to the front of
the freezer shelf.

Unfortunately, Magellan forgot his manners overnight.

When Magellan awoke he was longing for a swim.

Elliot drew him a deep tub of cold water.

He left Magellan diving and holding his breath.

"ELLIOT!"

Elliot rushed to the door.